DISCARD

I Want a Hippopotamus for Christmas

I Want a Hippopotamus for Christmas

Words and Music by *John Rox* · Illustrated by *Bruce Whatley*

HarperCollinsPublishers

Library of Congress Cataloging-in-Publication Data
Rox, John.
   I want a hippopotamus for Christmas / by John Rox ; illustrated by Bruce
Whatley.— 1st ed.
      p.   cm.
   Summary: An illustrated version of the song about a child who wants a
hippopotamus for Christmas.
   ISBN 0-06-052942-3 — ISBN 0-06-058549-8 (lib. bdg.)
   [1. Children's songs, English—Texts.   2. Hippopotamus—Songs and music.
3. Christmas—Songs and music.   4. Songs.]   I. Whatley, Bruce, ill.   II. Title.
PZ8.3.R7975Iw 2005   2003011028
[782.42]—dc22   CIP
                                                                          AC

Typography by Al Cetta and Jeanne L. Hogle
1   2   3   4   5   6   7   8   9   10
❖
First Edition

For Ruth, Adam, Rosie, and Lily
—B.W.

I want a hippopotamus for Christmas,

a hippopotamus is all I want.

Don't want a doll, no dinky Tinkertoy, I want a hippopotamus to play with and enjoy.

I want a hippopotamus for Christmas, I don't think
Santa Claus will mind, do you?

He won't have to use our dirty chimney flue, just bring him through the front door, that's the easy thing to do.

I can see me now on Christmas morning, creeping down the stairs. Oh, what joy and what surprise when I open up my eyes to see my hippo hero standing there.

I want a hippopotamus for Christmas, only a hippopotamus will do. No crocodiles or rhinoceroses, I only like hippopotamuses and hippopotamuses like me too.

I want a hippopotamus for Christmas,
a hippopotamus is all I want.
    Mom says a hippo would eat me up, but then
Teacher says a hippo is a vegetarian.

I want a hippopotamus for Christmas, the kind I saw last summer in the zoo.

We got a car with room for two in our two-car garage, I'd feed him there and wash him there and give him his massage.

I can see me now on Christmas morning creeping down the stairs. Oh, what joy and what surprise when I open up my eyes

to see my hippo hero standing there.

I want a hippopotamus for Christmas,
only a hippopotamus will do.
No kangaroos or duckbill platypuses,
I only like hippopotamuses

and hippopotamuses like me too,

Words and Music by John Rox

Brightly and lightly

I WANT A HIP - PO - POT - A - MUS FOR CHRIST - MAS, _____ A hip-po-pot - a - mus is all I

want. _____ Don't want a doll, _____ no dink - y Tink - er - toy, _____ I want a hip - po -
{Mom / Pop} says a hip-po _____ would eat me up, but then _____ Teach - er says a

pot - a - mus to play with and en - joy. _____ I WANT A HIP - PO - POT - A - MUS FOR CHRIST - MAS, _____ I
hip - po is a veg - e - ta - ri - an. _____ I WANT A HIP - PO - POT - A - MUS FOR CHRIST - MAS, _____ The

don't think San - ta Claus will mind, do you? _____ He won't have to use _____ our
kind I saw last sum - mer in the zoo. _____ We got a car with room for two in

dir - ty chim - ney flue, _____ Just bring him through the front door, that's the eas - y thing to do. _____
our two car ga - rage, _____ I'd feed him there and wash him there and give him his mas - sage. I can

DISCARD